GREAT ILLUSTRATED CLASSICS

THE PICTURE OF DORIAN GRAY

Oscar Wilde

adapted by
Fern Siegel

Illustrations by
Pablo Marcos

**BARONET
B O O K S**

BARONET BOOKS, New York, New York

GREAT ILLUSTRATED CLASSICS

edited by
Joshua E. Hanft

BARONET BOOKS is a trademark of Playmore Inc., Publishers
and Waldman Publishing Corp., New York, New York

Printed in the United States of America

Contents

About the Author

Oscar Wilde was born in Dublin, Ireland in 1854. He was an author, playwright, and wit. He was known for preaching the importance of style in life and art and for attacking 19th-century Victorian narrow-mindedness.

At 20, Wilde left Ireland to study at Oxford University. He was an outstanding student and won a prize for his poem "Ravenna." After college, he moved to London where he became prominent in social and literary circles.

He was an early leader of the Aesthetic Movement, which believed in the concept "Art for Art's Sake." He lectured on this in England and also the United States. Wilde charmed the Americans, who were initially suspicious of this eccentric Englishman.

Oscar Wilde landed in New York. When a customs officer asked if he had anything to declare, he replied: "I have nothing to declare but my genius."

The period of his great success began in 1888 when he published *The Happy Prince.* Oscar Wilde's only novel, *The Picture of Dorian Gray,* is a moral fable.

Though he wrote books, Oscar Wilde is best known for his plays: *Lady Windermere's Fan*, *An Ideal Husband*, and *A Woman of No Importance*, all written in the late 1890s. His stage masterpiece, *The Importance of Being Earnest*, is a play noted for its epigrams (clever sayings).

In 1895, at the age of 39, Wilde was at the peak of his career. He had three hit plays running at the same time in London. That same year he brought a libel action against the Marquis of Queensbury. The trial became a social scandal and Wilde eventually lost his case. He was sentenced to two years in prison.

From his prison experiences, he wrote his best poem, *The Ballad of Reading Gaol.* On his release, Wilde left England. Ruined in health and finances, and drained of creative energy, he died in France three years later.

An Important Painting

Chapter 1

The Fateful Meeting

Basil Hallward's London studio was filled with the smell of roses. The light summer wind stirred in the trees in his garden. Through the door came the heavy scent of lilacs. Basil was a painter and he loved to surround himself with beautiful things.

He had been working on an important painting and had invited his friend, Lord Henry Wotton, to visit. Lord Henry was also a lover of beauty and, at the moment, was admiring the portrait Basil had done. The painting was of a young man about 20. His name was Dorian Gray and he was very handsome. Lord Henry was extremely impressed by his friend's talent. As the painter admired his own work, a smile of pleasure came to his rugged face.

"It is your best work, Basil, the best thing you have ever done!" Lord Henry exclaimed. "You must send it to the Academy."

As the painter looked at the gracious figure he had captured in his painting, the smile passed from his face. Then he closed his eyes and placed his fingers upon the lids, as though he was in deep thought.

After a few minutes of silent contemplation, Basil spoke. "I don't think I shall send it anywhere." He frowned, shaking his head.

"Not send it anywhere?" questioned Lord Henry. "Have you any reason? What odd chaps you painters are! You would do anything in the world to gain a reputation. But as soon as you have one, you want to throw it away. A portrait like this could make you famous," he added,

"Your Best Work!"

hoping to impress his friend.

"I know you will laugh at me, Harry, but I can't. I have put too much of myself in it," Basil said.

"But, Basil," Lord Henry laughed, raising his eyebrows and staring at him in amazement. "I can't see any resemblance. You are rugged with dark hair, this young man is blond and fair. I don't see the problem. I didn't know you were so vain, Basil. But you flatter yourself. You don't look at all like Dorian Gray."

"You don't understand me, Harry," his friend sighed. "Of course I am not like him. I should be sorry to be so. There is a destructive quality about all such physical beauty. It is better not to be so different from others."

"Basil, I was wondering. How did you meet Dorian Gray?" asked Lord Henry.

"I went to a party at Lady Brandon's. You know we poor artists have to show ourselves in society from time to time just to remind the

"I Can't See Any Resemblance!"

public we aren't savages." Basil smiled. Then he continued. "After about ten minutes I ran into Dorian Gray. It was funny but from the moment Lady Brandon introduced us, I found him to be a most fascinating person. I had a strange feeling about our meeting—I knew he would have an impact on my painting."

Basil insisted that, thanks to Dorian Gray, his recent paintings were the finest he'd ever done and stated that Dorian's personality had suggested a whole new style of art. "Yet I'm sure Dorian Gray will suffer because of his good looks."

Lord Henry was very surprised by Basil's gloomy prediction. He was eager to learn more about this mysterious young man. When he heard all this, Lord Henry wanted to meet Dorian Gray. And, although Basil was reluctant to introduce them, Lord Henry got his wish, as he was still in the studio when Basil's butler announced, "Mr. Dorian Gray to see you, sir."

"Mr. Dorian Gray to See You, Sir."

The painter suddenly looked at Lord Henry with a very serious expression on his face. "Dorian Gray has become my dearest friend, Harry," he said. "Don't try to spoil him or influence him. Your influence would be bad."

If only Lord Henry had taken his advice!

The butler showed Dorian Gray into the room. The young man immediately sat at the piano, turning over the pages of a Mozart sonata. Both Basil and Lord Henry were struck by his features. He was certainly handsome, with blue eyes and gold-colored hair. He had an aura of purity and youth that enveloped him.

But Basil worried that Lord Henry would corrupt him.

"You must lend me this sheet music, Basil. I want to learn it. It is beautiful," Dorian announced.

"That depends on how you sit for me today, Dorian," Basil replied.

"Oh, I'm tired of sitting and I don't know if I

14

An Aura of Purity and Youth

want a life-sized portrait of myself," Dorian answered, swinging around on the music stool in a willful manner. When he caught sight of Lord Henry, he stopped at once. "I beg your pardon, Basil, I didn't realize you had company."

"This is Lord Henry Wotton, Dorian, an old Oxford friend of mine. I have just been telling him what a terrific subject you are," Basil said.

"I have a great pleasure in meeting you, Mr. Gray," said Lord Henry, stepping forward and extending his hand. "My aunt has often spoken to me about you. You are one of her favorites."

"I am on Lady Agatha's bad list at present," replied Dorian. "I promised to go to a club in Whitechapel with her last Tuesday and I genuinely forgot all about it. We were suppose to play a duet together—three duets, I believe."

"I will make peace with my aunt. She likes you very much." Lord Henry looked at him and was again struck by his handsome features and his youth. Dorian Gray seemed curiously

"A Great Pleasure in Meeting You"

unspoiled by the world. He seemed to be good and pure.

It was at that moment that Lord Henry decided not to pay attention to Basil's warning. And, although Basil had cautioned Dorian about Lord Henry's scandalous reputation, Dorian ignored him as well.

Lord Henry's words had a profound impact on the young, impressionable Dorian. He listened excitedly as Lord Henry began to explain his theory of beauty.

"To me, beauty is the wonder of wonders. It is only shallow people who do not judge by appearances," grinned Lord Henry. He looked at the young man. "Dorian, the gods have been good to you. But what the gods give, they quickly take away. You have only a few years in which to live. Then your youth goes—and your beauty will go with it. Then you will discover that there are no more triumphs left for you."

Dorian frowned slightly at these words. But there was more to come.

Listening Excitedly!

"We Never Get Our Youth Back!"

Chapter 2

A Wish Is Granted

"Realize your youth while you still have it,"
Lord Henry commanded. "One day, time will
catch up with you. You will become old and
gray. There is such a little time that youth will
last. The common hill flowers wither, but they
blossom again. But we humans never get our
youth back. Our limbs fail, our senses go," he
said, painting a scary picture for Dorian of old
age.

"We degenerate into a hideous old age,
haunted by the memory of missing out on passions that frightened us and temptations we

never yielded to. Don't squander your golden days. Live life! Search for new sensations! Be afraid of nothing!"

Dorian listened intently, wide-eyed and silent. Basil also heard these dangerous words and worried about the impression they would make on his inexperienced young friend. But he was too busy putting the finishing touches on Dorian's painting to warn him or to stop Sir Henry.

He stood staring at the picture for a long time, biting the end of one of his huge brushes and frowning. "It's finished," he said proudly at last. Then stooping down, he wrote his name in long red letters on the left-hand corner of the canvas.

"I congratulate you, Basil," Lord Henry said. "This is the finest portrait of any man that has been created in modern times. Dorian, come look at yourself!"

Dorian looked at the painting and blushed. The sense of his own beauty hit him like a

"It's Finished!"

lightning bolt. When he saw it, he drew back and his cheeks flushed for a moment with pleasure. A look of joy came into his eyes, as if he had seen himself for the first time.

Yet, a chill suddenly ran through him. One day he would be old and wrinkled, his slender form would be gone, and his hair would fall out.

"How awful it is," Dorian mused. "I shall grow old and horrible and dreadful. But this painting will remain always young. If it were only the other way! If only I were to be always young and the picture grew old. For that—I would give everything! I would give my soul!"

The painter stared in amazement. It was so unlike Dorian to think and speak like that. What had happened to him? Was Lord Henry's evil influence already at work?

"I am jealous of everything whose beauty does not die," said Dorian bitterly. "I know now that when one loses one's good looks, one loses everything. Your picture has taught me that.

"If Only I Were Always Young!"

Lord Henry is right. Youth is the only thing worth having. When I find that I am growing old," he cried, "I shall kill myself!"

Basil was stunned by what he heard, but before he could speak, Dorian shouted, "I am jealous of my portrait. It mocks me, Basil. I hate it! Why did you paint it?" With that, he flung himself onto the studio sofa and burst into tears.

"This is your doing, Harry," said Basil angrily.

Lord Henry shrugged his shoulders. "It is the real Dorian Gray. That is all."

Dorian barely heard Basil's charge against Lord Henry. He watched as the painter reached for a knife to rip the painting to shreds.

"Don't, Basil!" cried Dorian. "It would be murder."

"I'm glad you finally appreciate my work," the painter said coldly.

"Appreciate it? I am in love with it, Basil. It

Reaching for a Knife

is a part of myself. I feel that," Dorian explained. "I didn't mean I wished you hadn't painted it."

"As soon as it dries, it will be framed and sent to you." Basil put down the knife and spoke more gently.

Finally, Dorian calmed down. He made plans to dine with Lord Henry. Basil begged him not to go, fearing that the older man's influence would destroy his all-too-trusting friend.

But Dorian did not heed his warning. And his life would never be the same!

To Dine with Lord Henry

Grumbling Over His Newspaper

Chapter 3

A Romantic Background

At noon the next day, Lord Henry strolled from Curzon Street over to the Albany Club to call on his Uncle George. The rough-mannered old bachelor had been in the diplomatic service, but was now retired. This elderly gentleman was a hero to his butler and a terror to most of his relatives. Still, Lord Henry enjoyed his company.

When Lord Henry entered the Albany Club, he found his uncle sitting in a brown hunting jacket, smoking a cigar and grumbling over the newspaper.

"Well, Harry," said the old man, "what brings you here?"

"Family affection, Uncle George. Also, I wanted to ask you something. What I want is information about a Mr. Dorian Gray," Lord Henry replied.

"Mr. Dorian Gray? Who is he?" asked Uncle George, knitting his bushy white eyebrows.

"That's what I've come to learn. Or rather, I know who he is. He is the last Lord Kelso's grandson. His mother was Lady Margaret Devereux. I want you to tell me about his mother. What was she like? Who did she marry?"

"Kelso's grandson!" echoed the old gentleman. "Of course, I knew his mother well. She was an extraordinarily beautiful girl and made all the men frantic by running away with a penniless young fellow, a corporal in the Army.

"The poor chap was killed in a duel a few months after the marriage. There was an ugly story about it. They say Kelso paid some Belgian brute to insult his son-in-law in public,

Killed in a Duel

and then shoot him afterwards in a duel. He was a crack shot. The young man never stood a chance."

"And what happened to his wife, Dorian's mother?" asked Lord Henry.

"He brought his daughter back with him and, I am told, she never spoke to him again. The girl died, too, died within a year. She left a son." Uncle George went on to explain that Dorian's grandfather, Lord Kelso and his mother had a great deal of money. And, that by law, Dorian would inherit the family estate, Selby. "Dorian Gray," he said, "will one day be a very wealthy man."

"Thanks for the information. I always like to know everything about my new friends," smiled Lord Henry.

After exchanging pleasantries, Uncle George asked his nephew where he was lunching. "At Aunt Agatha's, both myself and Mr. Gray. He is her latest protege."

Uncle George growled approvingly and rang

"Dorian Gray Will Be a Wealthy Man."

the bell for his servant. He bid his nephew goodbye. Lord Henry walked into Burlington Street and turned his steps in the direction of Berkeley Square.

So that was the story of Dorian Gray's parents! Lord Henry was stirred by the romance and tragedy. A beautiful woman had risked everything for a mad passion! A few wild weeks of happiness cut short by a treacherous crime! The poor woman endured months of agony and then her child was born.

She was snatched away by death, the boy left alone and to the tyranny of an old and loveless man. Yes, thought Lord Henry, it was an interesting background. Dorian Gray was the son of love and death.

Stirred by Romance and Tragedy

Patiently Waiting

Chapter 4

Dorian Gray Falls in Love

One month later, Dorian Gray was sitting in an antique chair in the library of Lord Henry's house in Mayfair, a wealthy section of London. It was the charming room of an educated gentleman.

Lord Henry had placed yellow tulips in large blue china jars and on the mantelpiece. Solid oak bookcases sat against the walls. Through the small leaded panes of the window streamed the apricot-colored light of a summer's day in the city.

Dorian was patiently waiting for his friend

to return. Lord Henry had a habit of keeping people waiting. He claimed he was always late on principle. He liked to say that punctuality was the thief of time. It was another one of his sayings that meant to show how different he was from most people.

"Sorry I'm late, Dorian. I was looking for a piece of old fabric in Wardour Street and had to bargain for hours. These days people know the price of everything and the value of nothing," Lord Henry sighed.

"Your wife stopped by while I was here," Dorian told him. Lord Henry and his wife, a rather flighty, over-dressed woman, led very separate lives. Lord Henry's contempt for marriage was well-known.

"Never marry a woman with blonde hair," stated Lord Henry firmly.

"Why, Harry?" asked Dorian.

"Because they are so sentimental," he answered, adjusting his tie. "My advice to you is never marry at all."

"Never Marry at All"

"Don't worry," Dorian laughed. "I won't marry. I'm too much in love. That is one of your sayings, Harry," he blushed, "and I am putting it into practice. Her name is Sibyl Vane and she is an actress and a genius."

"Tell me about your genius," Lord Henry prodded. "How long have you known her?"

Dorian was very excited. He said that Lord Henry was responsible for his happiness, that his eccentric friend had filled him with a desire to know life. So Dorian searched all over London for new experiences.

He went everywhere—to fashionable museums and grimy back streets—looking for adventure. From St. James Park to Piccadilly Circus, Dorian sought new sensations. "I felt this London of ours must have something in store for me," he said, "with all its sinners and its sins.

"I remember that first evening we had dinner, Harry. You said the search for beauty was the real secret of life. So I took your advice and

Looking for Adventure

went searching for beauty.

"This is what happened," explained Dorian happily. "I was passing a funny little theater with great flaring gasjets and ugly playbills. A strange man stood outside it, wearing an amazing waistcoat and smoking a cigar.

"He led me to a small private box where I could watch the stage in peace. It was a third-rate curtain, colored in cupids and flowers. Women were selling oranges and ginger-beer and nuts," he added.

Dorian went on and on, describing *Romeo and Juliet*, the Shakespearean drama he watched, and how badly the orchestra played. Then, he said, he saw a beautiful young actress take the stage and, in an instance, he found passion and romance. Her voice was wonderful and her beauty unmatched. He had fallen in love immediately with actress Sibyl Vane.

"I am not surprised, Dorian, but is this the great romance of your life?" Lord Henry wondered. "You will always be loved and you will

A Young Actress

always be in love. A grand passion is the privilege of people who have nothing to do," he said, his eyes twinkling. "Still, I am curious. How did you meet her?"

"It happened the third night I went to the theater," replied Dorian. "I ran into that man again. He turned out to be Sibyl's manager. He had some connection with the theater, but insisted that the critics hated him. I had thrown Sibyl flowers one night and she had looked up at me. The old man noticed and decided to introduce me to her. I'm so glad he did!"

"What is your actress like?" asked Lord Henry.

"She is seventeen years old, with dark-brown hair, violet eyes and sweet lips. She is the prettiest thing I have ever seen in my whole life!" exclaimed Dorian. "She means everything to me. Every night I go to see her act and every night she seems to me better than the night before.

"She is so shy and gentle. Sibyl flatters me

"She Looked Up at Me!"

and says I am like a prince. Since she doesn't know my real name," he added, "she calls me Prince Charming."

Lord Henry watched his friend in amazement. How different he was from the quiet boy he had first met in Basil's studio! Dorian was growing up. He had matured and was enjoying his first love affair.

"I want you and Basil to come see Sibyl act," Dorian insisted, his eyes sparkling. "Once you see her perform, you'll appreciate her talent. I intend to rent a proper West End theater and introduce her to all the important critics. I will make my beloved Sibyl a star."

Lord Henry paused to take in Dorian's story. "Let me see. Today is Tuesday, let's meet tomorrow at the Bristol at eight o'clock. I'll bring Basil with me."

"Not eight, Harry. Let's meet at six. We must be at the theater before the curtain rises. Now I must go. Goodbye for now."

As he listened to Dorian's words, Lord Henry

"She Calls Me Prince Charming."

was conscious—and the thought brought a gleam to his brown eyes—that it was through certain words of his that Dorian Gray had fallen in love with this girl. To a large extent, he had encouraged Dorian's romantic nature. Sometimes books have a great influence. Sometimes it is a person. Lord Henry realized that he had had a great influence on the character and charm of Dorian Gray.

But who was this mystery woman who had captured Dorian's heart? Intrigued by Sibyl Vane, Lord Henry longed to meet her. The two friends parted, after agreeing to watch Sibyl perform the following night.

Later, Lord Henry sat by himself, thinking about Dorian's new-found passion. He marveled at the mysteries of love and attraction as he glanced at the scene outside his window. The sun was setting and the rooftops of the city glowed like plates of hot metal. The sky above was like a faded rose.

Lord Henry wondered what life had in store

The Two Friends Parted.

for his friend. But before he could speculate any more on the future, he got a surprise. It was a telegram from Dorian. It announced that he and Sibyl Vane were engaged to be married!

A Surprising Telegram

"Mother, I Am So Happy!"

Chapter 5

The Vane Family
Learns of the Affair

Sibyl's family was stunned by the engagement and eager to meet her young suitor. Her mother was initially upset. She had dreamed of Sibyl becoming a great actress. Marriage was not in her plans for her daughter.

"Mother, I am so happy!" whispered Sibyl, burying her face in the lap of the faded, tired-looking older woman. Her back was turned to the harsh light and she was sitting in a chair in their dingy parlor.

Mrs. Vane winced and put her thin white

hands on her daughter's head. "Happy!" she echoed. "I am only happy, Sibyl, when I see you act. You must not think of anything but your acting. Mr. Isaacs has been very good to us and we owe him money."

The girl looked up and pouted. "Money, Mother?" she cried, "what does money matter? Love is more than money!"

"What do you know of this young man? You don't even know his name! However, as I've said before, if he is rich ... " Mrs. Vane let her suggestion hang in the air.

"Mother, how can you think about money? I can only think about love," Sibyl said, her eyes sparkling. Yes, if Sibyl made a good match, it could help further the family's position in society, thought Mrs. Vane. So she had only one question for her smitten daughter: Was the young man rich? Sibyl, who sang the praises of her fiance, Prince Charming, assured her mother that he was a fine young gentleman, both wealthy and wonderful.

Was the Young Man Rich?

At that moment, the door opened and a young lad with rough brown hair came into the room. James Vane, Sibyl's brother, was stocky. His hands and feet were large and somewhat clumsy in movement. He was not as finely bred as his sister.

Nor was James as easily impressed as his greedy mother. He was very attached to Sibyl. He feared that her fiance, a rich and carefree fellow, was just playing with her affections. Why would such a man, who could keep company with a well-bred society lady, he wondered, marry a woman from the lower classes?

James Vane looked into his sister's face with tenderness. "I want you to come for a walk with me, Sibyl. I'm off to Australia tomorrow and I don't suppose I shall ever see this horrid London again."

"I'll change my clothes and meet you in a few minutes," Sibyl replied as she mounted the stairs.

"Oh, James," cried his exasperated mother,

Very Attached to Sibyl

"I wish you would stay here and get a job as a clerk in an office. Lawyers are a very respectable class, and in the country often dine with the best families. It pains me that you are leaving for Australia. I don't think there is any kind of society in the colonies."

"I hate offices and I hate clerks," he replied. "I have chosen my own life. All I ask is that you watch over Sibyl. Don't let her come to any harm. Mother, you must protect her."

"James, you talk so strangely. Of course, I will watch over our Sibyl."

"I hear a gentleman comes every night to the theater and goes backstage to talk to her. What about that?"

Mrs. Vane quickly explained to James that she had no doubt the young man was a perfect gentleman. "He is always most polite to me," she said, "and he looks rich and cultured."

"You don't know his name, though," said James harshly.

"No," admitted his mother with a placid ex-

"Watch Over Our Sibyl"

pression on her face. "He has not yet revealed his real name. He is probably a member of the aristocracy. And if he is wealthy, there is no reason," slyly suggested Mrs. Vane, "why Sibyl should not marry him."

James Vane bit his lip. "Watch over Sibyl, mother," he said again, "please watch over her."

"My son, you distress me very much. Sibyl is always under my special care. If this man is a gentleman and wealthy, there is no reason why she should not wed. He has the appearance of an aristocrat.

"I must say, it would be a brilliant marriage for Sibyl. They would make a charming couple. His good looks are really quite remarkable. Everybody notices them."

James muttered something to himself and drummed on the window with his fingers. He had just turned around to speak when the door opened and Sibyl ran in.

"How serious you both are!" she cried. "What

"How Serious You Both Are!"

is the matter?"

"Nothing," James muttered, "I suppose one must be serious sometimes. Goodbye, mother. I will have my dinner at five o'clock. Everything is packed."

"Come, Sibyl," added her brother, "let's go for our walk now." They went out into the flickering, wind-blown sunlight and strolled down the dreary Euston Road. The people passing by glanced at the unusual couple—a sullen, heavy youth and a graceful, refined-looking girl. James was like a gardener walking with a rose.

Sibyl, however, was quite unaware of the effect she was producing. She was smiling, thinking of her Prince Charming and how much she longed to see him again. Her brother James was also thinking about her suitor.

"You have a new friend, I hear. Who is he? Why have you not told me about him? He means you no good," snarled James.

"Stop, Jim!" she exclaimed. "You must not

"He Means You No Good!"

speak against him. I love him!"

"Why, you don't even know his name!" answered her brother. "Who is he? I have a right to know!"

"He is called Prince Charming. Don't you like the name? If you only saw him," said Sibyl, "you would think him the most wonderful person in the world. When you come back from Australia you will meet him. I wish you were coming to the theater tonight. He is going to be there."

"I want you to beware of him," warned James. He insistently expressed his concern for Sibyl's happiness. "If your Prince Charming ever hurts you," he growled, "I swear I will kill him!"

"I Swear I Will Kill Him!"

"Dorian Gray is Engaged to be Married!"

Chapter 6

Lord Henry and Basil
Discuss the Engagement

"I suppose you have heard the news, Basil?" asked Lord Henry that evening. Basil was being shown into the private room at the Bristol where they were having dinner.

"No, Harry," answered the artist, giving his hat and coat to the bowing waiter. "What is it?"

"Dorian Gray is engaged to be married," said Lord Henry, watching his friend carefully as he spoke.

Basil started and then frowned. "Dorian engaged to be married! It is impossible!"

69

"It is true," said Lord Henry.

"To whom?" Basil wanted to know at once.

"To some unknown actress," he replied.

"I can't believe it!" said Basil. "Dorian is far too sensible."

"Dorian is far too wise not to do foolish things now and again, Basil," Sir Henry proclaimed.

"Marriage is hardly a thing one can do now and again," Basil reminded his friend.

"But I didn't say he was getting married. I said he was engaged. There is a difference," smiled Lord Henry in his peculiar way.

"But think of Dorian's birth and position and wealth!" declared Basil. "It would be absurd for him to marry a girl who wasn't from his class."

"If you want to make him marry this girl, tell him that, Basil. He is sure to do it then," Lord Henry admonished.

"I hope the girl is good, Harry," sighed Basil.

"She is better than good—she is beautiful,"

"To Marry a Girl Not from His Class"

murmured Lord Henry, sipping a glass of wine.

"She may be very beautiful, Harry, but I still don't want to see Dorian tied to a bad woman," Basil stated firmly.

"You will see for yourself tonight. We are to see her at the theater. Dorian is joining us here and then taking us to meet her."

"But do you approve of it, Harry?" asked the painter, walking up and down the room and biting his lip. "It is probably just some silly childish infatuation."

"I never disapprove or approve of anything now," Lord Henry noted. "It is Dorian's decision."

Just then, Dorian himself entered. He threw off his evening cape and shook hands with both his friends.

"Harry, Basil, you both must congratulate me. I have never been so happy." Dorian was flushed with excitement and pleasure and he looked very handsome.

Flushed With Excitement

"I hope you will always be very happy, Dorian," said Basil. "How did you decide to propose to the young lady so quickly?"

Dorian told the two men that it had happened the previous night. "After I left you yesterday, Harry, I dressed, ate dinner at an Italian restaurant in Rupert Street and went to the theater. Sibyl was performing that night and was wonderful. She is a born artist. I sat in the dingy box, enthralled. I forgot that I was in London in the nineteenth century.

"When the performance was over, I went behind and spoke to her. As we were sitting together, there came a look into her eyes. My lips moved towards hers. We kissed. She trembled. It was the most perfect moment of my life," Dorian said quietly.

"Of course, our engagement is a deep secret. I don't know what my guardians will say. All I know," he said, "is that I love Sibyl Vane and I want the world to know she is mine.

"And there is something else, Harry. When

"We Kissed!"

I am with Sibyl I regret what you have taught me. I become a different man with her. The man who could wrong her would be a beast, a beast without a heart. She makes me good. When we are together, I forget all your evil, poisonous ideas," Dorian declared.

"And those are...?" asked Lord Henry, helping himself to some dessert.

"All your theories about life," Dorian replied. With that, the men ended their discussion. They finished dinner and put on their coats. A doorman hailed a carriage to take them to the theater.

Hailing a Carriage

A Fat Manager

Chapter 7

A Great Disappointment

Lord Henry and Basil were more anxious than ever to meet Sibyl Vane as they rode with Dorian in the elegant carriage to the run-down theater.

The two men were curious about the young beauty who had captured Dorian's heart. Would they be as infatuated with her as he was? Or was Dorian throwing away his chance to find a more suitable wife?

A fat manager with jeweled hands escorted them to their seats. Suddenly, amidst a round of applause, Sibyl Vane stepped onto the cramped stage. Yes, she was certainly lovely to look at, Lord Henry thought, one of the loveliest women he had ever seen. The scene was from *Romeo and Juliet* and all the shabbily-dressed actors were on stage. Then, Sibyl Vane appeared. Her body swayed while she danced. Her hands seemed to be made of cool ivory.

The three men watched her perform a famous scene from the play. It was a very dramatic, moving moment, one Sibyl had done many times. Each time, she had captivated her adoring audience. But tonight, for some strange reason, Sibyl seemed dull and listless. She showed no signs of joy when, as Juliet, her eyes rested on Romeo. Her words were spoken in an artificial manner.

She acted very badly and Dorian Gray grew pale as he watched her. Basil and Lord Henry just dismissed her performance as of someone inexperienced. True, she looked charming, but her acting was terrible. When the second act was over, there came a storm of hisses.

She Acted Very Badly.

Lord Henry got up from his chair and put on his coat. "She is quite beautiful, Dorian, but she cannot act. Let us go."

Sibyl's failure to impress the audience troubled Dorian deeply. He felt humiliated in front of his best friends. "I'm sorry you both had to waste an evening," he apologized. "She is a commonplace, mediocre actress."

"Don't talk like that about anyone you love, Dorian," Basil cautioned. "I should think Miss Vane was ill. Love is more important than art."

"Don't worry about it, Dorian," advised Lord Henry. "I don't suppose you will want your wife to act after you are married so what does it matter? Come to the club with Basil and me and we will toast to the beauty of Sibyl Vane."

But Dorian could not be consoled by his friends and he asked them to leave. "Go away!" he cried. "My heart has been broken."

He sat through the remainder of the show, then rushed to Sibyl's dressing room. The girl stood there with a look of triumph on her face.

Humiliated in Front of His Friends

Her eyes were lit with fire. There was a radiance about her.

"How badly I acted tonight!" she cried.

"Horribly," he answered. "It was a dreadful performance. Are you ill?"

"I shall never act well again," she mused. "You don't understand, do you? Before I knew you acting was the only reality in my life. Tonight, for the first time, I saw the sham, the silliness of the theater.

"You gave me something better. You made me understand what love is. You are more to me than any play could ever be! My love! My Prince Charming! You mean everything to me!"

"But don't you realize what you have done? You have killed my love for you," Dorian coolly replied. He looked at her harshly.

"I loved you because you were great. Because you had such talent. Instead, I find you are shallow and stupid. What a fool I was! I will never see you again!" he screamed in anger.

"You Have Killed My Love."

Sibyl became frightened. How could her Prince Charming be so mean to her? He had said he loved her, he had kissed her and promised her the world. Why had he changed so? Sibyl started to cry and, as she fell to the floor, she grabbed Dorian's knees, clutching at him for dear life.

"Please don't be cruel to me, dearest. I will work hard and try to improve myself. I promise you I will be a better actress next time. I love you so much. Please don't leave me," she begged.

Dorian looked down at her with angry eyes. His upper lip curled in disdain. He became hard and brutal. Her tears did not melt his icy heart. He flung Sibyl aside and turned on his heel.

"I'm going," he said in a calm, clear voice. "I can't see you any more. You have bitterly disappointed me." With that, he stormed out of the theater.

Hard and Brutal

The Face Had Changed.

Chapter 8

The Horror Begins

Dorian wandered around Covent Garden for hours that night, upset and confused. Huge carts filled with flowers rumbled slowly down empty streets. He watched the farmers unload their wagons. All the while, he was racked by pain and disappointment. In the morning, tired and exhausted, he returned to his mansion.

As he opened the door, his eyes fell on the portrait Basil Hallward had painted of him. He was startled by what he saw. The face appeared to have changed! Was such a thing possible? It was strange, but the expression *was* different—there was a touch of cruelty in the mouth that had not been there before.

Could he be dreaming? Dorian examined the painting more closely. He opened the blinds. The bright dawn light flooded the room. The strange expression on the painting remained. He picked up a mirror and examined his own face. His features were the same—only the mouth of the painting was distorted.

He wasn't dreaming. It was horrible! What did it mean? He threw himself into a chair to think. Suddenly, he remembered the words he had spoken in Basil's studio the day the painting was finished.

He had made a crazy wish: He asked to remain young and for the portrait to grow old. Now, his mad desire had come true. Dorian's face would remain young and handsome and the canvas would bear the burden of his sins!

But such things were impossible. It seemed monstrous to even think of them. And yet, there was the picture before him—with that

Picking Up a Mirror

definite touch of cruelty in the mouth.

Dorian, a selfish man, thought only of his own destiny. He did not think about the pain he had caused Sibyl Vane. Instead, he reserved his pity for a great work of art. He was saddened that its beauty had changed.

He suddenly realized that this scary painting held the secrets of his life! It told his story. It had changed already. Its gold would wither into gray. Its color and fire would die. It was terrible! For every sin that he committed, his portrait would pay the price. What had he done? Would a painting teach him to hate his own soul?

Frightened by this mystery, Dorian resolved never to sin again. He would resist temptation. He would not see Lord Henry any more, not listen to his poisonous theories.

Dorian decided that he would go back to Sibyl Vane, make his apologies and marry her. He realized that he had been selfish and cruel to Sibyl. But he would make it up to her. They

His Portrait Would Pay the Price.

would be happy and their life together would be beautiful and pure.

Dorian Gray got up from his chair and drew a large screen right in front of the portrait, shuddering as he glanced at it. He walked to the door and opened it. When he stepped out on the grass, he grew a deep breath. The fresh morning air seemed to drive away all his demons. His thoughts were only of Sibyl when he went to bed at last.

The Fresh Morning Air

Looking Over His Letters

Chapter 9

A Rude Awakening

It was long past noon when he awoke. Victor, his French valet, had crept several times on tiptoe into the room to see if he was stirring. Finally, his bell sounded, and Victor came in quietly with a cup of tea and a pile of letters.

After a few minutes, Dorian got up, threw on a cashmere bathrobe and went into the bathroom. The cool water refreshed him and he seemed to forget the argument of the previous night. He returned to his bedroom, sipped some weak tea, and looked over his letters.

One was from Lord Henry, and had been

brought by messenger that morning. He hesitated, then put it aside. The others he opened. They contained the usual assortment of invitations to dinner, tickets to private art showings and programs for charity concerts.

Suddenly, his eye fell on the screen that he had placed in front of the portrait. Was it all true? Had the portrait really changed? Or had it simply been his over-active imagination that had made him see a look of evil where there had been a look of joy? Surely a painting could not change.

He knew that when he was alone, he would have to examine the portait. When the coffee had been brought, Victor left the room. Then Dorian rose from the bed and threw himself down on a Spanish couch that stood facing the screen.

What if by some fate or deadly chance someone else should see the horrible changes? What would he do if Basil wanted to see his picture again? Dorian got up and locked both

Had the Portrait Really Changed?

doors. At least he would be alone when he looked upon his mask of shame. Then he drew the screen aside and saw himself face to face. It was perfectly true. The portrait had changed!

It was incredible! How could such a thing occur? Was there some connection between the picture painted on the canvas and the soul that was within him? He gazed at the picture in sickened horror and fear.

Dorian realized that one thing the changed portrait had done was to make him see how unjust, how cruel he had been to Sibyl Vane. It was not too late to make amends. She could still be his wife. His selfishness would be transformed into some nobler passion.

Finally, he decided to write a letter to Sibyl, to beg her forgiveness, to say how much he loved her. As he finished his letter, there was a knock at the door. His servant announced that Lord Henry was anxious to see him. Without waiting for permission, Lord Henry rushed

Horror and Fear

into Dorian's bedroom.

"I'm so sorry, Dorian," Lord Henry began.

"Do you mean about Sibyl Vane?" Dorian asked.

"Did you go see her after the play?" his friend inquired.

"Yes, and I was brutal to her," admitted Dorian. "But I'm better now. I have decided that from now on I will be good. I want to marry Sibyl. I'm going to go see her today and ask her to forgive me for my terrible behavior."

"It's too late!" cried Lord Henry. "Sibyl Vane is dead!"

A cry of pain broke from the Dorian's lips and he leaped to his feet. "Dead! Sibyl dead! It is not true! It is a horrible lie! How dare you say it?"

"It is quite true, Dorian," said Lord Henry gravely. "It is in all the morning papers. I wrote to you this morning to ask you not to see anyone until I came. There will be an inquest of course, and you must not be mixed up in it.

A Cry of Pain

There would be a terrible scandal if you were. Do they know your name at the theater?" he asked. "If they don't, it's all right. Did anyone see you going to her dressing room last night? That is important."

Dorian did not answer for a few moments. He was dazed with horror. Finally, he stammered, in a stifled voice, "Harry, I can't bear it! Please tell me everything that happened."

"I Can't Bear It!"

Lying Dead on the Floor

Chapter 10

Sibyl Commits Suicide

Lord Henry explained that as Sibyl was leaving the theater with her mother, she claimed to have forgotten something in her dressing room. When she didn't come back down, the stage manager went to get her. He found her lying dead on the floor. She had swallowed some poison and died instantly.

"I have murdered Sibyl Vane," Dorian said, hanging his head in shame, "murdered her as surely as if I had cut her little throat with a knife."

Lord Henry consoled his friend, insisting

that Sibyl was an overly-romantic girl who had taken her own life. No one was to blame, he said.

Dorian listened to Lord Henry's words. He felt the time had come to make up his own mind.

Or had the choice already been made? Life itself had decided for him. Eternal youth, passion, wild joys and wilder sins—these things would be his.

"Oh, Harry, how I loved her once! It seems years ago to me now. She was everything to me. Then came that dreadful night—was it really only last night—when she acted so badly, and my heart broke.

"She explained it all to me. But I wasn't moved a bit. I thought Sibyl was shallow. Then something happened that made me afraid. I can't tell you what it was," he said, thinking about the strange painting. "But it decided for me. I would go back to Sibyl."

Lord Henry listened to his friend without

Consoling Words

speaking. He found the suicide a dramatic interlude at best; in truth, he cared only for Dorian's reputation.

"Harry," cried Dorian Gray, coming over and sitting beside him, "I don't feel this tragedy. Am I heartless?"

"No, you are only very young and very romantic. In time, you will recover. Come with me to the opera tonight, it will help you to forget," Lord Henry counseled.

Dorian quickly accepted the invitation. He vowed not to think about Sibyl again. To Dorian, his own happiness would be all that mattered. He would quickly forget about the dead Sibyl Vane.

"You have helped me through a bad time, Harry. I wonder what life has in store for me now," he said.

"Life has everything in store for you, Dorian. There is nothing that you, with your extraordinary good looks, your charm, and your resources, will not be able to do."

The Opera Tonight

Strong words, yet a feeling of pain crept over Dorian as he thought of the desecration in store for his portrait. Now it would become a monster! The shame of it all would have to be hidden away!

For a moment he thought of praying that the horrible connection that existed between him and the picture might end. It had changed in answer to a prayer. Perhaps a new prayer might undo the old one.

But Dorian did not pray. He could not give up the chance to remain forever young. This portrait would be the most magical of mirrors.

If only he hadn't been so foolish and so vain! His life would never be the same!

Desecration of His Portrait

Offering Sympathy

Chapter 11

Basil Almost Discovers
the Dreaded Secret

The next day Basil Hallward came by to see Dorian. He wanted to offer his sympathy about Sibyl's death. He also wanted to ask his friend if he would let him exhibit his portrait in a Paris gallery.

Dorian was eating lunch when Basil was shown into the room. "I read of Sibyl in the late edition of *The Globe* I picked up at my club. I came here at once," said Basil. "I can't tell you how sorry I am. I know you must feel terrible. Did you go down and see the girl's mother?"

"Of course not," murmured Dorian Gray, as he sipped yellow wine from a Venetian glass and looked bored. "I was at the opera."

"You went to the opera!" exclaimed Basil, shocked at Dorian's callous behavior. "You went to the opera while Sibyl Vane lay dead?"

"Stop talking about it!" cried Dorian. "What is past is past."

"You call yesterday the past?" asked his horrified friend. "Dorian, this is horrible. Something has changed you completely. You talk as if you had no heart, no pity. It is all Harry's bad influence."

Dorian brushed away Basil's words with a wave of his hand. "I don't want to be at the mercy of my emotions. A man who is master of himself can end a sorrow as easily as he can invent a pleasure. I want you to draw me a picture of Sibyl, Basil. I should like to have something to remember her by."

"All right," Basil agreed, "if it would please

"Something Has Changed You!"

you. But you must then do something for me. Please come to my studio and sit for another portrait."

"I can never sit for you again, Basil. It is impossible!" Dorian swore angrily.

The painter stared at him. "Don't be ridiculous. Don't you like the painting I did of you?" Basil asked. "Why have you pulled the screen in front of it? It is the best picture I have ever done. It is disgraceful of you to hide my work away."

"The light was too strong on the portrait," Dorian hastily explained.

"Too strong! Surely not. It's a great place to hang it. Let me see it." Basil walked towards the corner of the room.

A cry of terror broke from Dorian Gray's lips and he rushed between the painter and the screen. "You must not look at it!"

"Why shouldn't I look at it?" asked Basil, laughing.

"If you try to look at it, Basil, on my word of

"You Must Not Look at It!"

honor, I will never speak to you again. I'm very serious."

Basil was thunderstruck and he looked at Dorian in absolute amazement. He had never seen him like this before. Dorian was actually pale with rage. His hands were clenched and he was shaking all over.

"I won't look at it if you don't want me to," he said coldly, turning on his heel and going over towards the window. "But really, it's strange I'm not allowed to see my own work, especially as I am going to exhibit it in Paris in the fall."

"To exhibit it! You want to exhibit it?" exclaimed Dorian, a great sense of fear creeping over him. Was the world going to be shown his secret?

"Why should you object?" asked Basil. "If you keep it behind a screen, you must not like it very much."

Dorian Gray passed his hand over his forehead. There were beads of sweat there. He felt

Pale with Rage

that he was on the brink of a terrible danger. "You can't have forgotten that you assured me that you wouldn't exibit the painting," cried Dorian. Then he remembered that Lord Henry had said to him once, half jokingly, that he should ask Basil why he would not exhibit Dorian's portrait before.

"Basil," he said, looking his friend in the eye. "What was your reason for refusing to exhibit my picture before now?"

The painter shuddered in spite of himself. "Dorian, if I told you, you would laugh at me. If you don't want me to see your picture, I won't ask again. Your friendship is more important to me than the painting."

"No, Basil, you must tell me," insisted Dorian. "I have a right to know." He was determined to find out Basil Hallward's mystery.

"Sit down, Dorian," said the painter, looking troubled. "And just answer me one question: Have you noticed something curious in the painting? Something that didn't strike you at

"Sit Down, Dorian!"

first, but was later revealed to you?"

"Basil!" screamed Dorian, clutching the arms of his chair and staring at him with wild eyes.

"I see you did. Don't speak," replied Basil. "Your personality had the most extraordinary influence over me. One day—a fatal day, I think—I decided to paint a portrait of you as you are. Whether it was the realism of the method or the wonder of your personality, something happened. I worked very hard and it was a great success. But I had put too much of myself into it. My praise for you was too great. So I decided not to allow the picture to be exhibited."

Basil continued. "It is amazing to me, Dorian, that you should have seen this in the portrait."

"I saw something," the young man answered slowly, "something that seemed curious."

"Well, then, " said Basil relieved, "you won't mind now if I exhibit the work."

"Basil!"

"Never," growled Dorian.

Basil decided not to argue with his friend and agreed to his odd request. "It's your decision and I respect it, Dorian. Goodbye for now. You have been the one person in my life who has really influenced my art."

Basil picked up his hat and coat and turned to his friend. "You will sit for me again?" he asked.

"Impossible!" Dorian said. "I can't explain it to you, Basil, but I must never sit for you again. There is something fatal about a portait. It has a life of its own."

He bid Basil goodbye and closed the door. Suddenly, Dorian Gray smiled to himself. He had succeeded in fooling his friend. Basil would never learn the truth about the awful portait. Still, he grew worried. The portrait must be hidden away at all costs. He could not run such a risk of discovery again!

"It Has a Life of Its Own."

Hiding His Tortured Painting

Chapter 12

An Evil Book
Changes Everything

The day after Sibyl's suicide, Dorian decided to hide his tortured painting. What if someone else saw it? What would they think? He ordered his servant to take the painting to the third floor of his townhouse and store it in his old playroom.

His trusted servant was given strict orders. No one was allowed to enter the room. Only Dorian had the key to unlock its thick wooden door. There, he thought, his dreadful secret would be safe from the world.

As the door closed, Dorian put the key in his pocket and looked at the room that would house his secret. His eyes fell on a large 17th-century purple satin cover his grandfather had found in a convent in Italy. Yes, that would serve to wrap the dreadful painting. It had often wrapped the dead. Now it would hide something that had a corruption of its own. Worse than the corruption of death—something that would breed horrors but would never die!

He turned, locked the door and went downstairs to his sitting room. He picked up the St. James *Gazette*. The newspaper was full of reports of Sibyl's death. Fortunately for Dorian, his name was never mentioned. Relieved that he had avoided any bad publicity, Dorian was once more determined to think only of his own pleasure in the future.

It was just after 5 o'clock when the doorbell rang. A messenger had a package from Lord Henry. To cheer Dorian up, Lord Henry had

Wrapping the Dreadful Painting

sent him a little yellow book. It was the strangest book Dorian had ever read in his life!

It chronicled all the sins of the world. The novel had no plot and only one character—a young Parisian man who spent his life trying to realize, in the nineteenth century, all the passions of every century before his own. It was a book of evil.

But Dorian was so fascinated that he could not stop reading. For years to come, Dorian Gray would never free himself from the influence of this evil book. He never even tried. Instead, he ordered no less than nine large-paper copies of the first edition from Paris.

He had them bound in different colors so they might suit his moods. The hero, a young Parisian in whom the romantic and scientific temperments blended, very much resembled Dorian Gray. The character was so much like him that this strange novel seemed to contain the story of his life—even before he had lived it!

A Strange Book

The good looks that had been captured in Basil's painting of Dorian captivated others as well. Even those who heard the most evil things about Dorian Gray could not believe them. He didn't look evil at all. Instead, he had the look of someone who kept himself pure.

Yet Dorian began to live the life written about in Lord Henry's book. And it was so easy. He was rich. His handsome features captivated everyone who met him. He knew joy and cruelty. He could have whatever he wanted.

Strange tales began circulating around London about him. He still looked pure, but was he? Dorian would disappear on long, mysterious absences. Afterwards, he would creep upstairs to the locked room and stand in front of the portrait that Basil had painted.

There, he would look at the evil, ugly, aging face on the canvas. He grew more and more taken with his own looks, and more and more interested in the corruption of his own soul!

No one knew where he went. No one knew

In Front of the Portrait

about the sordid room in the nasty tavern near the docks. Traveling in disguise and under an assumed name, Dorian Gray would frequent this awful place.

All the sins he had read about in the little yellow book became real to him. With wild abandon, Dorian Gray fed his mad hunger for adventure and destruction! He indulged his every mood, every whim, every want. He mined the deep mysteries of all the senses.

At the same time, Dorian was known as a man-about-town. He was famous for dressing well. He was rich and indulged his every whim. He began to collect musical instruments, expensive jewels, and beautiful works of art. He had a house in London and a huge estate in the country.

He spent his money recklessly.

But all these treasures, everything he collected, were just a means of escape. Hanging on the walls of the lonely locked room where he had spent his childhood, he had hung the

Traveling in Disguise

terrible portrait whose constantly changing features showed him the real degradation of his life.

He had draped the purple and gold Italian curtain over it to hide it from view. For weeks he would not go to the locked room and he'd forget the hideous painted thing. For a time, he would enjoy a light-hearted and joyous existence.

Then, suddenly, at night he would creep out of the house, and go to dreadful places near Blue Gate Fields and stay—day after day—until he was driven away. On his return, he would sit in front of the picture—somtimes hating it and himself. After a few years, he could not bear to be parted from the painting for long periods of time. He gave up the villa he had shared with Lord Henry in Italy and the little white house in Algiers where they would spend the winter.

Dorian Gray worried about the painting that was now such a part of his life. What if it

The Real Degradation

was stolen? Or what if, while he was away, someone gained access to the rooom, in spite of the bars, and learned his secret! The very thought terrified him. What if the world already suspected?

After all, there were people who distrusted him. He was nearly blackballed at a West End club. Once, when he was brought by a friend into his London club, the Duke of Berwick and another gentleman got up and left!

By his 25th birthday, wild stories were again circulating in polite society. It was said that Dorian Gray had been seen fighting with foreign sailors, that he kept company with thieves and other criminals.

Women who had adored him, now shunned him. Respectable men would leave the room if he entered their club. What had happened to the once innocent boy? Only Dorian Gray knew the answer. He had been poisoned by Lord Henry's book.

To him, evil was now beautiful.

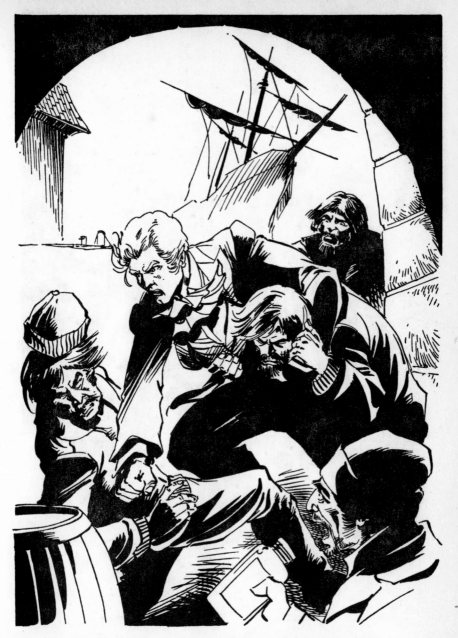

Fighting with Foreign Sailors

A Man with a Bag

Chapter 13

Basil Tries To Save His Friend

Thirteen years later, on the ninth of November, on the eve of his 38th birthday, Dorian was walking home. He had dined at Lord Henry's and the night was cold and foggy.

At the corner he passed a man with a bag in his hand. Dorian recognized Basil Hallward. A strange sense of fear, which he did not understand, came over him. He did not want to speak to Basil, so he pretended not to recognize him. Dorian walked quickly in the direction of his house.

But Basil had spotted Dorian and placed his

hand on Dorian's arm. "Dorian! I have been waiting for you in your library. I'm off to Paris by the midnight train. I'll be gone for six months. I wanted to speak to you before I left. I thought it was you. But I wasn't sure. Didn't you recognize me?"

"In this fog, Basil? Why, I can't even recognize Grosvenor Square. I'm sorry that you are going away, I haven't seen you for ages."

"Here we are," said Basil. "I really must speak to you. It is most important."

"All right. You'd better come in," said the weary Dorian.

Basil followed Dorian into the library. There was a bright wood fire blazing in the large open hearth. Brandy and soda stood on a table nearby.

"I can't wait any longer, Dorian. There is something I must say to you," Basil stated.

"What do you want to talk about, Basil?" asked Dorian. "I'm very tired and I want to go to bed."

"I Must Speak to You."

"It's about you. I think you should know that the most terrible things are being said against you in London. Your reputation is in ruins," said Basil sadly.

"I don't care what other people gossip about," replied Dorian, and he sighed. "I only care about other people's scandals."

"You must care, Dorian. Of course, I don't believe the horrible things people say. I think sin is something that writes itself across a man's face. It cannot be hidden. You look as young and pure as you did when we first met.

"Yet I see you very seldom," he continued, "and I hear such hideous things. Why do so many gentlemen refuse to go to your house or invite you to theirs? Why is your friendship so fatal to other people?" Basil ticked off a list of prominent men who had been ruined by Dorian Gray.

He mentioned a young royal son who had committed suicide in the Navy, Lord Kent's son who married a prostitute, and the scandal